Captain Flinn
and the
Pirate Dinosaurs

Written by
Giles Andreae

Illustrated by
Russell Ayto

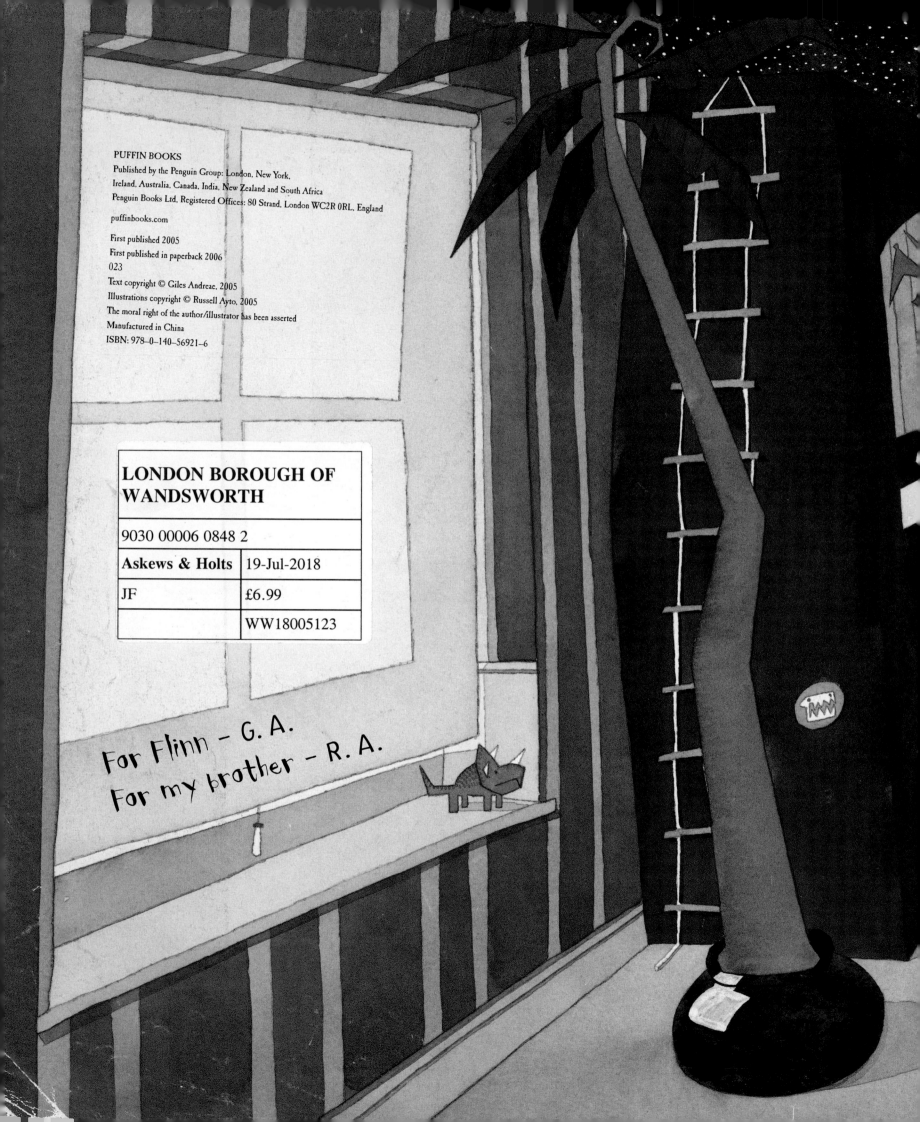

PUFFIN BOOKS

Published by the Penguin Group: London, New York,
Ireland, Australia, Canada, India, New Zealand and South Africa
Penguin Books Ltd, Registered Offices: 80 Strand, London WC2R 0RL, England

puffinbooks.com

First published 2005
First published in paperback 2006
023

Manufactured in China
ISBN: 978–0–140–56921–6

For Flinn – G. A.
For my brother – R. A.

This is Flinn.
He is wearing his pirate T-shirt and
colouring in a picture he has drawn of a dinosaur.
Flinn LOVES dinosaurs.

One day at school, Flinn was colouring in a new
dinosaur picture when he realized he didn't have
quite enough pens.

"Why don't you have a look in the art cupboard, Flinn?"
said Miss Pie, his teacher. "I think there are
more colours at the back."

So Flinn opened the door
and stepped
into
the
cupboard.

There were lots of paints and rolls of paper and pots of glue, but Flinn couldn't see any pens.

As he searched, he heard a noise.

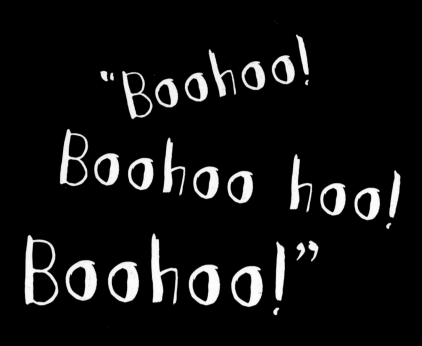

"Boohoo!
Boohoo hoo!
Boohoo!"

and then,

"Sniffle,
snuffle,
sniffle."

Right at the back of the cupboard,
under an old curtain, was something
shaking and shuddering
like a giant jelly.

Flinn crept closer and closer. When he
lifted up the curtain . . .

he couldn't believe his eyes!

It was a real live
PIRATE CAPTAIN!

"Hello," said Flinn. "What's the matter?"

The pirate, whose name was Captain Stubble,
sniffed and looked at Flinn.

"My ship! They've stolen my ship!"
he sobbed. "One minute I was fast asleep and
the next I was in the water watching my
precious ship, the *Acorn*, sail away."

   "But who has stolen it?" asked Flinn.

   "I don't know," said Captain Stubble,
"but as I watched I heard a . . .

ROAR!

...And then a strange kind of song.

It went: 'Yo ho ho!
Yo ho ho!

Somethingy,
something –

Go! Go! Go!'"

"Hmmm, very strange," said Flinn. "How will you get your ship back?"

"I don't know," blustered Captain Stubble. "I can't do it on my own!"

"I could help," said Flinn bravely.

"And so will we!" It was Flinn's friends, Pearl, Tom and Violet.

"We love adventures!" they said.

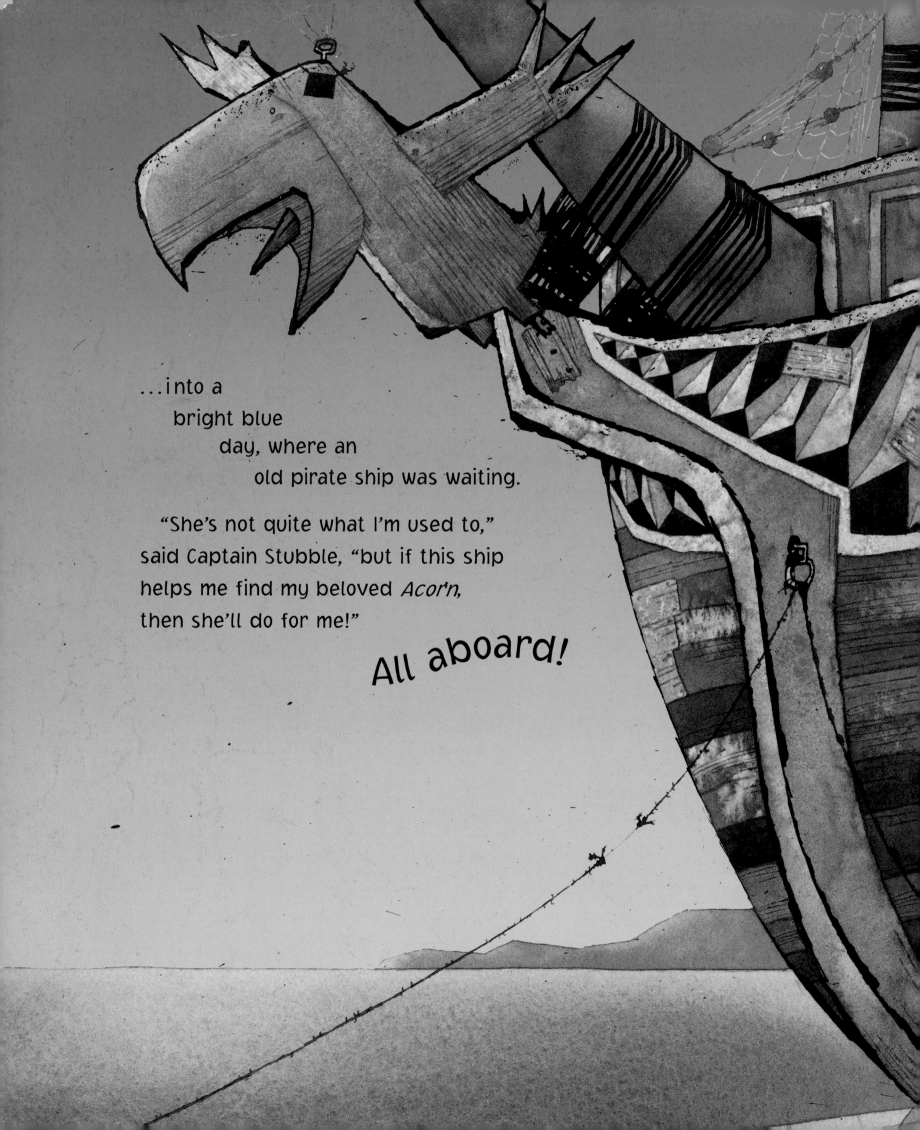

...into a
    bright blue
        day, where an
            old pirate ship was waiting.

"She's not quite what I'm used to,"
said Captain Stubble, "but if this ship
helps me find my beloved *Acorn*,
then she'll do for me!"

All aboard!

"Right, me hearties," said Captain Stubble, "if you're going to be pirates, you'll need to look like pirates."

Flinn brandished a gleaming silver cutlass.

"And since you seem to be so brave, Flinn," he said, "you can be Captain of this ship. I'd much rather be the cook."

So Captain Flinn took over

and they sailed . . .

...and sailed...

in search of the *Acorn*.

The pirates were about to give up hope, when Pirate Violet shouted from the crow's-nest,

"SHIP AHOY!"

Stubble grabbed his telescope.
"That's my precious *Acorn*!" he cried.
"LET'S BOARD IT!" cried Captain Flinn.
"And reclaim your ship from those pirate baddies! ALL HANDS ON DECK!"

They sailed faster and faster and got closer and closer.

When they were nearly alongside, Captain Flinn put the telescope to his eye. His face went white. "They're not just **ordinary** pirates," he stammered, "they're...

"...PIRATE DINOSAURS!"
And that is exactly what they were.

There was a pirate diplodocus...

a pirate stegosaurus...

a pirate triceratops...

and a pirate pterodactyl!

And, right at the helm of the ship, steering its course with his claws on the wheel, was a
GREAT...BIG...PIRATE...

When he saw
Captain Flinn he
roared an almighty

ROAR!

The dinosaurs sang out
in their terrible voices:

"Yo ho ho!
Yo ho ho!
Pirate
Dinosaurs
Go! Go! Go!"

...the
Tyrannosaurus
Rex!
He roared
an almighty

ROAR!

Captain Flinn could see his
huge sharp yellow teeth, and
his tonsils wobbling ferociously
at the back of his throat.
"I challenge you to a duel!"
shouted Captain Flinn.

"I'm going to cut you up into little pirate sausages!" yelled the Tyrannosaurus Rex, dribbling greedily. "Then I'm going to put you on the barbecue and

EAT YOU UP!

With much too much tomato ketchup!" he added.

"Oh no, you're not!" yelled Captain Flinn, and charged.
Their cutlasses FLASHED and CRASHED and BASHED and SMASHED

for at least two hours and
twenty-five minutes until,
finally,

the Tyrannosaurus Rex
was **exhausted.**

"Captain Flinn," he stammered, "I surrender.
You are such a great pirate that YOU should
be the captain of all the Pirate Dinosaurs!
Please spare me and I promise I'll be the
goodest goody in the world. Honest!"

"Then maybe one day I will be your captain," replied Captain Flinn, "but now we'd better get back to school. It's almost lunchtime!"

So Captain Flinn took the wheel of the *Acorn*.
And while Pirate Pearl, Pirate Tom and Pirate Violet
untied the crew, Stubble made a delicious shark's-fin stew.

When they got to the harbour, they waved goodbye to Captain Stubble and to the Tyrannosaurus Rex.

Flinn saw that the door they had fallen through was still hanging open. So they all clambered in . . .

...and instantly they were back among
the paints and rolls of paper and pots of glue.
Flinn grabbed some colouring pens and
they all crept back into the classroom.

"And they all lived happily ever after," said Miss Pie, closing
the book she had been reading. "You've been in that cupboard
a long time, Flinn. What *have* you been doing?"

Flinn smiled secretly at his friends.

"Oh nothing," he said.
"Nothing really at all."